The Tinder Box

Retold by Russell Punter

Illustrated by Annette Marnat

Tinder boxes were used to start fires before matches were invented.
Inside the box was a flint, a piece of steel and some cloth (tinder).
You hit the steel with the flint to make sparks which set light to the tinder.
The tinder was then used to light a candle.

Trooper Tom was marching home from battle when...

Rustle

Rustle

out from the bushes sprang...

...an old woman.

"Would you like to be wonderfully rich?" she croaked.

"Of course," said Tom, "but how?"

"Below that hollow tree you'll find a cave," the woman explained.
"Inside are three treasure chests.
But be warned! A fierce dog guards each one."

Lay the dogs on
my apron and they
won't harm you.

"All I want is the old tinder box that's down there," she added.

"Will you help me?"

"Okay!" agreed Tom.

He lowered himself into the glowing depths,

down...

and down...

and down...

At the bottom was a cave, lit by a swarm of shimmering fireflies.

"The treasure must be behind those doors," thought Tom.

"Not to mention the growling guard dogs!"

The first door opened with a creepy creeeeak.

Trembling, Tom
tiptoed inside.

Grrrr!

There, on a treasure chest, sat a **huge** dog,
with eyes as big as tea cups.

Tom carefully lifted the dog onto the apron.

Then he tugged open the chest.

Easy, boy.

Wow!

A stream of shiny copper coins cascaded out.

"I'm rich!" said Tom.

In the second room he found...

an **enormous** dog
with eyes as big as saucers.

Tom set him down
on the apron and
opened the chest.

Sparkling silver
spilled out.

"Hurray! I'm **really**
rich," cried Tom.

Nice doggy...

Next door, a **gigantic** dog with eyes as big as dinner plates was on guard.

Tom heaved him onto the apron and opened the chest.

Glittering gold flooded onto the floor.

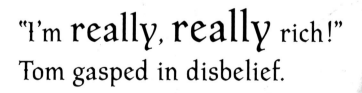

"I'm **really, really** rich!" Tom gasped in disbelief.

Tom was about to leave, when he remembered
the tinder box.

Ah, there it is!

He grabbed the box and climbed outside.

As Tom handed over the tinder box,
a firefly fluttered from his backpack.

Noooo! Fireflies
are deadly
to me.

It landed on the old
woman's nose, and...

WHOOSH!

She vanished
in a puff of smoke.

Tom was shocked.
"Poor thing," he said.

There was nothing he could do, so Tom clanked off to town with his treasure.

He stayed in swanky hotels

and splashed out on fancy clothes.

But Tom was too kind-hearted.

He shared his fabulous fortune,

until, at last...

...every penny was gone.

All Tom had left was the tinder box.

I'm f..f..freezing!

"I'll light a candle to keep warm," he thought,
and he struck the steel with the flint.

Pop! A dog with eyes as big as tea cups appeared.

What is your wish, master?

You're the dog from the cave! Do you grant wishes?

"I could really use some money," said Tom, slightly dazed.

The dog bounded off and swiftly returned with a bag of gold... and then another... and another.

Tom moved into a grand house in the town.
One day, the king and queen rode by.

Why does no one go
out to cheer?

"Nobody likes that snooty
pair," sniffed his maid.

"They keep the poor
princess locked up so
no one can see her."

Hmmm...

That evening, Tom summoned the dog.

"Please bring the princess here," he commanded.

When he saw the beautiful princess,
Tom fell head-over-heels in love.

At daybreak, the dog returned her to the palace.

"I have a feeling the princess was out last night," said the king.

"We'll soon know if it happens again," said the queen.

She tied a bag of flour with a hole in it to her daughter's nightgown.

Now the princess left a tell-tale trail behind...

The next morning, the king followed
the trail to Tom's house.

"Caught you!" he roared.
"No one may see the princess."

You'll die
at dawn
tomorrow!

Tom was tossed into the palace dungeon.

"I'll never set eyes on the princess again," Tom sighed.

Just before dawn, his maid came to say goodbye.

Suddenly, Tom had an idea.

"Please rush home and fetch my tinder box," he whispered.

At the crack of dawn, Tom was marched into the town square.

The townsfolk felt sorry for the poor soldier.

"Quiet, peasants!" snapped the queen.

Shame!

Spare him!

Let him go!

"Yes, silence!" barked the king. "Or you'll be next."

Now's my chance...

Tom plucked the tinder box from his pocket.

He struck the steel three times and POP! ZAP! POW!

All three dogs from the cave sprang into action.

"Chase the king and queen from the kingdom!" ordered Tom.

Grrrr!

Call them off!

Help!

Tom set the princess free and asked her to marry him.

Their wedding was a day of celebration across the land.

The crowds cheered.

Tom's maid wept tears of joy.

And the three dogs looked on
patiently, without barking once.

About the story

The Tinder Box was first written by Hans Christian Andersen
nearly two hundred years ago. The son of a Danish shoemaker, Andersen
wrote many classic stories including 'The Emperor's New Clothes'
and 'The Little Mermaid'.

Edited by Lesley Sims

First published in 2015 by Usborne Publishing Ltd., Usborne House, 83-85 Saffron Hill,
London EC1N 8RT, England. www.usborne.com Copyright © 2015 Usborne Publishing Ltd.